Land of the WILD LLAMA

A Story of the Patagonian Andes

by Audrey Fraggalosch
Illustrated by Michael Denman & William Huiett

For my brother Grant — A.F.

To our children and grandchildren — M.D. & W.H.

Text copyright © 2002 Audrey Fraggalosch.
Book copyright © 2002 Trudy Corporation.

Published by Soundprints Division of Trudy Corporation, Norwalk, Connecticut.

Book layout: Marcin D. Pilchowski
Editor: Laura Gates Galvin
Editorial assistance: Chelsea Shriver

First Edition 2002
10 9 8 7 6 5 4 3 2 1
Printed in Singapore

Acknowledgments:
Our very special thanks to Julie Ann Jarvinen, faculty member of the College of Veterinary Medicine of Iowa State University in Ames, Iowa, for her curatorial review.

Library of Congress Cataloging-in-Publication Data is on file with the publisher and the Library of Congress.

Land of the
WILD LLAMA

A Story of the
Patagonian Andes

by Audrey Fraggalosch
Illustrated by Michael Denman & William Huiett

Soundprints
Where Children Discover...

A giant bird sails over the towering, snow-capped peaks of the Andes Mountains in Patagonia. It glides with gusts of strong wind, rarely flapping its huge five-foot wings. Below on the grasslands, it spots a herd of guanacos. The condor swoops down and lands near a female guanaco with a newborn baby by her side. The guanaco quickly drives the condor away, protecting her baby from the huge scavenger.

Meanwhile, another female in the guanaco herd stands quietly as she gives birth, dropping her baby feet first onto the ground. It wobbles on its long legs, as it tries to stand up. Then, the newborn nuzzles up and down his mother's side, searching for her warm milk. The baby's coat is still damp, but the soft, woolly fiber will soon dry out in the warm sun.

Within fifteen minutes, the baby guanaco, or chulengo, can walk and keep up with his mother. Chulengo's herd includes eight female guanacos and their young. They are led by his father, a large male who protects the family from danger.

In a few weeks, Chulengo is strong enough to jump and neck-wrestle with other youngsters in the herd. He romps and darts about, strengthening his muscles for a life on the run.

Over the next few months, Chulengo begins to graze, nipping off grasses and chewing on the leaves of small shrubs. Through the grasses, he suddenly sees a pair of long legs rushing by. Startled, Chulengo moves closer to his mother as a flock of ostrich-like birds hurries past with their swarm of chicks. The giant rheas zigzag through the grasses and bounce off into the distance. Behind them, the bushy tail of a gray fox disappears like a puff of smoke.

On a nearby ridge, Chulengo spots his father frozen in stillness. His father's enormous dark eyes glare at an approaching male guanaco. The guanaco challenges Chulengo's father to a fight. His father spits back in defense. He then rears up on his hind legs and rushes at the intruder. *Thunk!* They slam chests together. Chulengo's father kicks and tries to bite the other guanaco's front legs. Twisting their long necks together, they push and shove at each other until Chulengo's father pushes the weaker guanaco down to his knees. The intruder limps away.

Triumphant, Chulengo's father leads his family to a small lake surrounded by lush grasses. They eagerly lap up the cool water after surviving for days on just the moisture from the plants they have eaten. Nearby, Chulengo hears the noisy gabbling of geese and the honking of buff-necked ibises. Just as he finishes his drink, a great flock of flamingos lands on the lake, turning it into one great mass of red and pink.

14

Now it is December and high summer in Patagonia. There is daylight for eighteen hours. The wind whistles wildly through the dry grasslands. Chulengo and his mother paw out a hole in the ground and then roll on their backs in the dusty hollow. Their thick coats become covered with dust. The dust helps keep them fluffy and dry.

After their dust bath, Chulengo and his mother rest in the shade of thorny thickets. Suddenly, Chulengo's father screams loudly, waking Chulengo with his alarm cry. In a split second, Chulengo is up! His heart pounds loudly as his father herds the family together and they race over the grasslands at high speeds.

Chulengo gallops as fast as he can to keep up with the rest of the herd. Finally, they reach the safety of a bluff. When Chulengo looks behind him, he catches sight of a big sandy-brown cat disappearing into the scrub. That was lucky! If his father had not spotted the mountain lion, it would have made a meal of Chulengo!

In June, winter comes to the mountain country. Now the jagged mountain peaks are covered with snow and ice. To keep warm, Chulengo and his mother huddle together. Their thick, brown coats insulate them from the cold. When snow covers the grasslands, it is hard for them to paw through the frozen surface to find grasses to nibble. Every day there is less and less to eat.

Finally, spring arrives in Patagonia. There are fresh grasses to eat and the joyful calls of meadowlarks float over the grasslands. Now Chulengo is one year old and no longer needs his mother. Soon she will have a new baby and Chulengo will leave his family.

Chulengo will roam for a while on his own. Then he will join a group of other males. In a few years, he will have a family of his own. And someday, Chulengo will be the leader of his own herd in the wild, windy mountains of Patagonia.

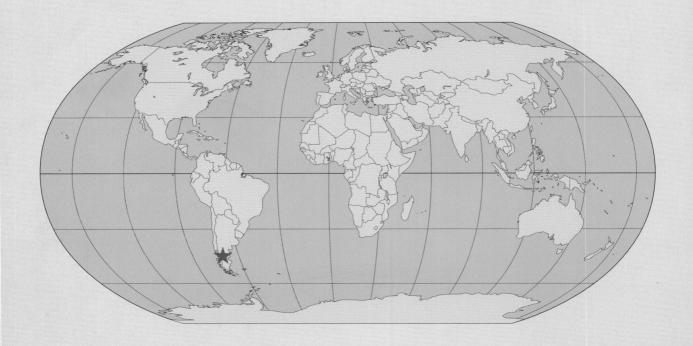

Chilean Patagonia, South America

Patagonia is a South American region that stretches across southern Argentina and southern Chile between the Andes Mountain and the Atlantic Ocean. The Andes, the longest uninterrupted mountain chain in the world, extend 6,000 miles down the backbone of South America. Chile is in the southern hemisphere, where winter occurs between the months of June and August and summer takes place between December and February.

About Torres del Paine, the Patagonian Andes

Declared a World Biosphere Reserve by UNESCO in 1978, Torres del Paine is one of the most rugged and remote places on earth. It is home to such varied wildlife as the guanaco, Chilean flamingo, Andean condor, rhea and mountain lion, among many other species.

The llama, alpaca, vicuna and guanaco are members of the South American camelid family living in the Andes Mountains. The llama and alpaca were domesticated over 4,000 years ago and are believed to be descended from the guanaco and vicuna. The vicuna, with its silky fleece, still lives in the coldest and highest regions of the Andes—between 13,000 and 16,000 feet. The guanaco, which resembles a small llama, ranges up to 13,000 feet, but also inhabits plateaus, grasslands and coastal lowlands.

Guanacos live in family groups, usually comprised of a single dominant male and up to ten females and their young. Newborn guanacos are called chulengos and can walk within minutes of being born. When they are no longer dependent on their mothers, yearlings are driven from the herd by the dominant male. Females eventually join the families of the adult males, while young males form separate packs. After three to four years, the males try to gather families of their own.

Once numbering in the millions, only about 100,000 guanacos survive today in all of South America. Beginning in the nineteenth century, intense hunting and severe habitat reduction decimated their population. Now both the vicuna and guanaco are protected species and are beginning to thrive in areas protected by law. Conservation efforts are essential to their survival.

Glossary

▲ *Guanacos*

▲ *Ovenbird*

▲ *Burrowing owl*

▲ *Mountain lion*

▲ *Chinchilla*

▲ *Pierid butterfly*

▲ *Plains viscacha*

▲ *Hairy armadillo*

▲ *Pampas grass*

▲ *Elegant crested tinamou*

▲ *Andean condor*

▲ *Torres del Paine*

 ▲ *Sword-billed hummingbird*

 ▲ *Copihue*

 ▲ *Andean goose*

 ▲ *Puna flamingo*

 ▲ *Buff-necked ibis*

 ▲ *Long-tailed meadowlark*

 ▲ *Grey fox*

 ▲ *Rhea*